For everyone and especially for Jack

for Carla!

And Vigo!

Stan Lee

Don't Dribble on the Dragon!

Written by Steven Lee
Illustrated by Shalini Vadivelu

My brother has a dragon and he keeps it secretly
Within a box beneath his socks,
He's hiding it from me.

It's not because I'm scared, you know,
It's not that I'm a thief.
It's just because my gums are sore from all these brand new teeth.

We used to have some fun before,
The dragon, Jack and me.

We used to play at cowboys
and I'd be his deputy.

Jack would be the sheriff and the dragon Pistol Pete
And together we would capture him beneath a giant sheet

But the moment that my teeth came through,
We'd load him on the wagon

and the only thing I'd hear from Jack was:
"Don't dribble on the dragon!"

One time we pretended to be spacemen lost in space
And the dragon was a baddie from some strange and alien race,

As he flew towards our spaceship getting ready to attack

accidentally dribbled and I got some drips on Jack.

The dragon laughed and so did I, the game came to an end.

hink that was the moment when I lost Jack as a friend.

I guess it's hard when you're thirteen and trying to be cool
To have a little brother with a face that's drenched in drool

But still I wished that things would change between

And we'd go back to how we were - one happy family.

And that's why as I say this I am climbing up the stairs,
While Jack is in bed sleeping I will catch him unawares.

The dragon has a plan, you see, to make us friends once more,
  cross my heart and hope it works

and open up the door.

And there he is, our dragon, sitting splendid on Jacks bed,
He's preparing to breathe fire and he's aiming at Jack's head!

I ring a bell to wake Jack up, Jack starts to scream and shout

But it's too late the flames pulsate...

Till my dribble puts them out.

"So sorry," says the dragon, "I did that in my sleep. Thank heavens for your brother!"

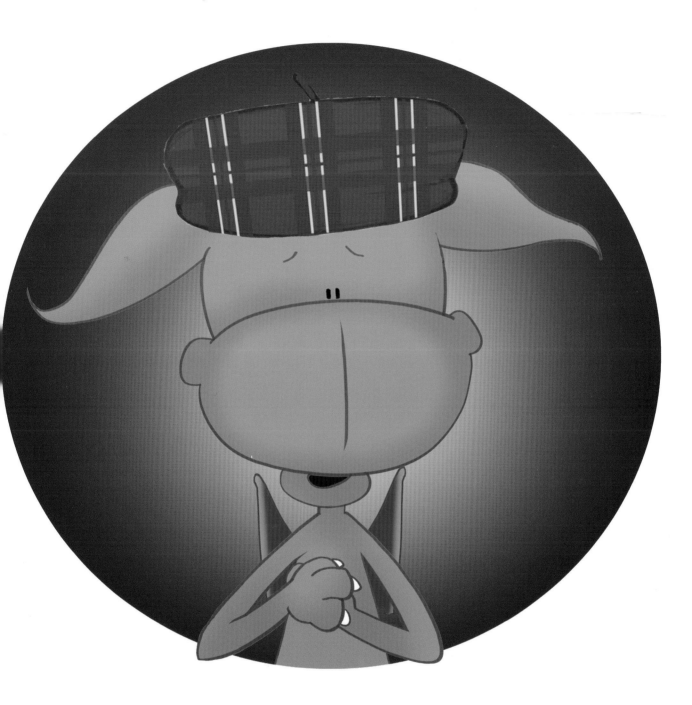

and then Jack begins to weep.

"I'm sorry too," he tells me, "I've been such an awful brother,
Oh please will you forgive me
(and please swear to not tell mother)."

Of course I promise Jack," I say, "I've always loved you best."
ack hugs me tight, with all his might,

In three days time we venture to his sock drawer Jack and me
But when we open up the box no dragon do we see

Instead a letter sat there says "I'm sorry that I've gone.
Two other brothers need me now to help *them* get along."

Years later Jack and I discussed the dragon in our past,

"I guess," he said, "some things in life are just not meant to last."

34

But even though we learnt that all good things must reach an end
I also learnt a brother...

Can be a boy's best friend.

The End

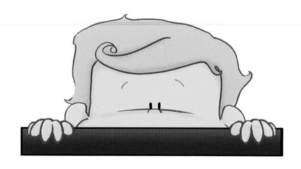

If you have enjoyed this book then Steven and
Shalini would love to hear from you.
You can write to them on the wall of the facebook
group The People's Theatre Company or get in touch
via twitter at @the_ptc